A NEW DAY

For Maureen, with love

First published in 2017
by Jessica Kingsley Publishers
73 Collier Street
London N1 9BE, UK
and
400 Market Street, Suite 400
Philadelphia, PA 19106, USA

www.jkp.com

Library of Congress Cataloging in Publication Data
A CIP catalog record for this book is available from the Library of Congress

British Library Cataloguing in Publication Data
A CIP catalogue record for this book is available from the British Library

ISBN 978 1 78592 308 1
eISBN 978 1 78450 617 9

Printed and bound in the United States

Manufactured by Thomson-Shore, Dexter, MI (USA); RMA17CS110, June, 2017

A NEW DAY

A STORY ABOUT LOSING SOMEONE YOU LOVE

FIONA MCDONALD

Jessica Kingsley *Publishers*
London and Philadelphia

Brown mouse feels sad.

Brown mouse is crying.

Brown mouse wants to be alone.

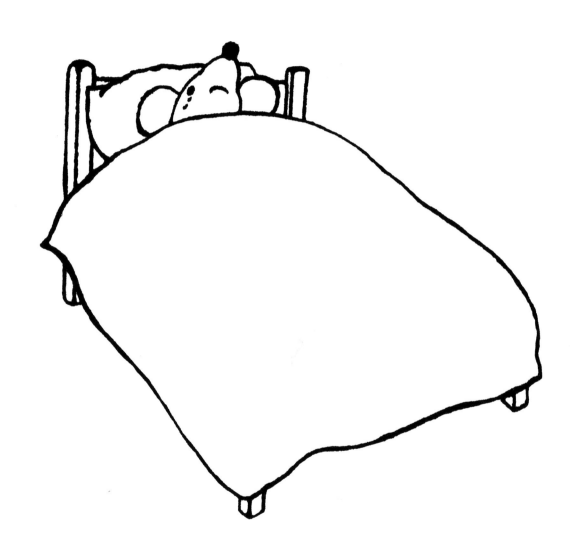

Amber mouse wants to help.

She brings tea and a cake.

Brown mouse says no.

Rose mouse wants to help.

She tries to read her a book.

Brown mouse says no.

Sunny mouse wants to help.

She has a beautiful blanket for her.

Brown mouse says no.

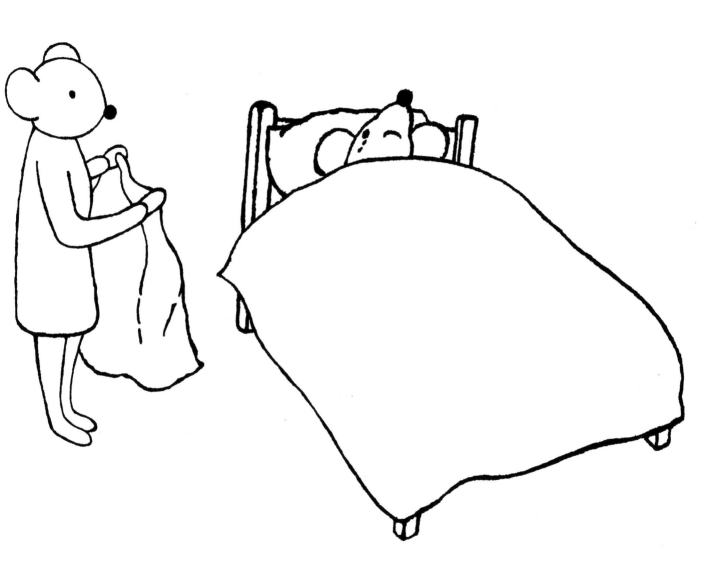

It's daytime but Brown mouse falls asleep.

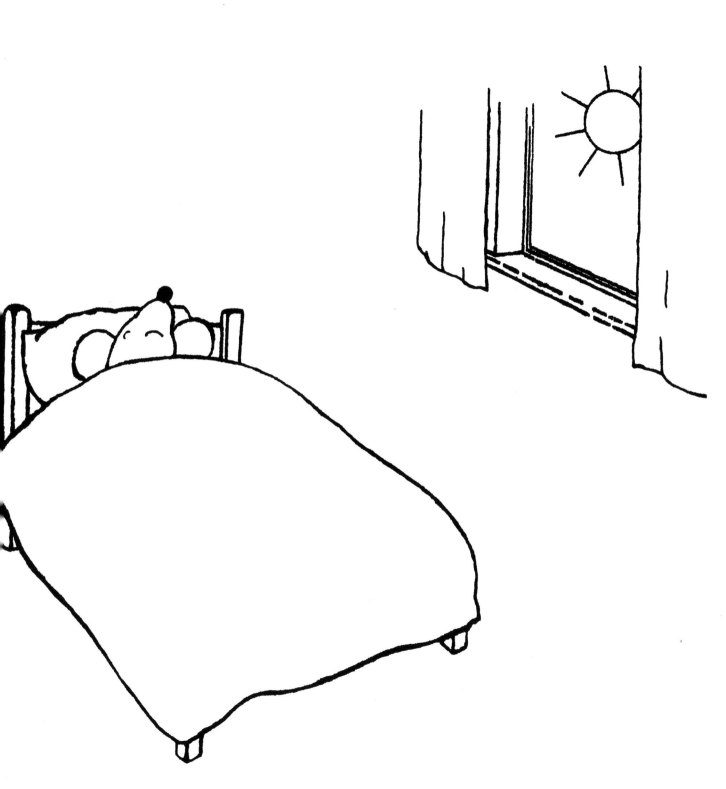

When she wakes up it is dark outside.

She walks through to the kitchen wrapped in Sunny's blanket and carrying Rose's book.

All the mice are sitting around the table drinking tea.

They are talking about Grey mouse.

Grey mouse has died.

All the mice are sad.

Brown mouse sits down at the table.

She sips some hot sweet tea and eats a cake.

The mice share memories of Grey mouse.

She was beautiful.

She was kind.

She had warm grey fur.

She smelt sweet.

She gave big hugs.

She had a huge smile.

She made lovely meals.

She made perfect tea.

She wore a cardigan with tiny buttons.

She got grumpy when the house was messy.

She fed the birds every day.

'I wonder where she is,' says Brown mouse.

'I hope she is sliding down rainbows in the sky, or lying under the warm sun, or floating on a cloud helping little mice learn things.'

The mice know that Grey mouse is not coming back.

'I think she is happy,' says Brown mouse.

All the mice smile. Outside the birds are singing and the sky is getting lighter.

'Let's feed the birds just like Grey mouse did,' says Amber mouse.

She reaches out her arm to Brown mouse and guides her to the door.

The sun is shining and the birds are singing. They step outside into the sunshine. It's a new day.

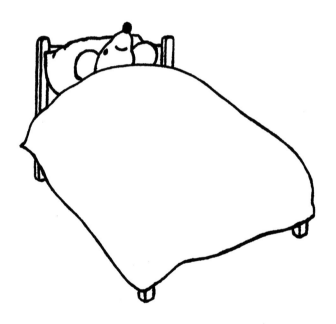